ready, ste

Swim, Sam, Swim

Leon Rosselson
Illustrated by Anthony Lewis

Puffin Books

PUFFIN BOOKS

Published by the Penguin Group
Penguin Books Ltd, 27 Wrights Lane, London W8 5TZ, England
Penguin Books USA Inc., 375 Hudson Street, New York, NY 10014, USA
Penguin Books Australia Ltd, Ringwood, Victoria, Australia
Penguin Books Canada Ltd, 10 Alcorn Avenue, Toronto, Ontario, Canada M4V 3B2
Penguin Books (NZ) Ltd, 182–190 Wairau Road, Auckland 10, New Zealand

Penguin Books Ltd, Registered Offices: Harmondsworth, Middlesex, England

Published in Puffin Books 1993
10 9 8 7 6

Text copyright © Leon Rosselson, 1994
Illustrations copyright © Anthony Lewis, 1994
All rights reserved.

The moral right of the author and illustrator has been asserted

Filmset in Monotype Bembo Schoolbook

Reproduction by Anglia Graphics Ltd, Bedford

Printed in England by Clays Ltd, St Ives plc

Sam looks glum. He can't swim.
Whoever heard of a frog that
can't swim?

All the other little frogs in the
swimming class can swim, at least
a few strokes.

But Sam can't swim. Not even
a few strokes.

This is what he *can* do. He can jump up and down in the water, yelling, "It's cold. It's cold."

He can smack his arms down hard on the water to scatter spray everywhere.

He can whoosh watery waves
over his older brother, Billy.

He can rest his mouth on the
surface of the water and blow
bubbles. But he can't swim.

"*Swim*, Sam, *swim*," says the swimming teacher. "Whoever heard of a frog that can't swim?

"Just do what I do. Move your arms like this and your legs like this. It's easy."

Sam copies what the swimming teacher is doing. He moves his arms like this and his legs like this, sinks to the bottom of the pond and comes up spluttering.

The swimming teacher scratches his head wonderingly. "Keep trying," he says. "That's the way to learn."

Sam looks at all the other young
frogs swimming around the pond.

Billy is sticking out his tongue.

Sam looks glum.

"When I was your age," says Sam's father that night, as he tucks Sam into bed, "my father took me to the river and threw me in. That taught me to swim, all right."

"Can't I learn to fly instead?"
asks Sam.

"Frogs don't fly," says Sam's
father.

"I could be the first flying frog,"
says Sam.

"The river," says his father.
"That's the place to learn to
swim."

So the next Sunday afternoon, Sam and Billy go off with their father and mother to a stony beach by the river. This is a favourite spot for swimming.

"Can I have a snail sandwich?" asks Sam.

"A swim first," says his father. And before you can say "Swim, Sam, swim", Father Frog is showing everyone how he can swim at top speed backwards and forwards across the river . . .

Sam's mother is cruising gently up
and down . . .

and Billy is paddling in the
shallow part of the pool.

But Sam is running along the
river bank, his arms outstretched,
pretending to be a bird.

"*Swim*, Sam, *swim*," says his father. "Whoever heard of a frog that can't swim?"

Gingerly, Sam steps into the shallow part of the river.

"Now," says Sam's father, "just do what I do. Move your arms like this and your legs like this. It's easy."

Sam copies what his father is doing. He moves his arms like this and his legs like this, sinks to the bottom, gulps down a bucketful of water and comes up spluttering.

"Oh dear!" says Father Frog,
scratching his head wonderingly.
"Never mind, Sam. Keep trying.
That's the way to learn."

"I'll never learn to swim," Sam
tells his mother as she gives him a
goodnight kiss.

"I can hop,

"I can jump,

"I can leap,

"I can skip,

"I can run,

"I can sit just as still as a stone,
but I'll never learn to swim."

"Of course, you will," says his
mother. "All frogs can swim."

"Do I have to be a frog?" asks
Sam.

"What would you rather be?"

"A lion," says Sam. "Can't I be
a lion?"

"I'm sure it's more fun being a
frog," says his mother.

"Not a frog that can't swim,"
sighs Sam.

"The lake," says his mother
with a far-away look in her eye.
"That's the place to learn to swim.
When I was a young frog, my
mother took me to the lake and
taught me to swim there. It was
lovely among the reeds, with the
wind making ripples on the water."

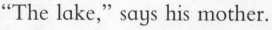

"I'd rather be a lion," says Sam.

"The lake," says his mother.
"You'll see."

The following Sunday, Sam and
Billy set off early with their father
and mother to spend the day at
the lake.

"Last one into the water's a silly
snail," says Sam's father.

Sam's brother and mother and father leap into the lake and are soon happily swimming and diving and floating.

But Sam sits at the side of the
lake and roars as loudly as he can.

"I'm a lion," he says. "Lions
don't swim."

"*Swim*, Sam, *swim*," says his mother. "Whoever heard of a frog that can't swim?"

"I'm not a frog," says Sam.

"Come on, Sam. Into the water," orders his mother.

Gingerly, Sam steps into the water at the very edge of the lake.

"Now," she says, "just do what
I do. Move your arms like this and
your legs like this. It's easy."

Sam copies what his mother is doing. He moves his arms like this and his legs like this, swallows a bathful of water and comes up spluttering.

"Oh dear!" says Mother Frog, patting him on the back. "Never mind, Sam. Keep trying. That's the way to learn."

At the end of the summer, all the
young frogs are gathered in the
pond to show their mothers and
fathers how well they can swim.

Up and down and round and
round they swim. All except Sam.
Sam looks glum. He still can't
swim.

All the young frogs form a circle
round Sam. "*Swim*, Sam, *swim!*"
they chant.

"Can't," says Sam. "Won't,"
says Sam. "I want to play."

"Play?" The swimming teacher
opens his mouth wide in surprise
and forgets to shut it again.

"Play?" Sam's mother and
father look at each other.

"Play?" The grown-up frogs
shake their heads sadly.

"Play?" The young frogs jump
up and down in the water, shaking
with laughter at the very idea.
"What do you want to play?"

"Dolphins!" yells Sam.

And suddenly he is diving under the water, paddling with his arms, twisting and turning and gliding and chasing imaginary fish, leaping high into the air then shooting under the water again, propelling himself along with his powerful legs.

Then he stands up, shakes the
water out of his eyes and sees all
the frogs staring at him in
astonishment.

"You could swim all the time,"
says the swimming teacher.

"That's not swimming," says
Sam. "That's playing dolphins."

"We want to play dolphins, too!" cry the other young frogs excitedly.

And soon the pond is busy and wavy with little frogs being dolphins, diving under the water, twisting and turning and gliding and chasing imaginary fish, leaping high into the air then shooting under the water again.

The swimming teacher looks
amazed. So do all the mother and
father frogs.

They scratch their heads and mutter to one another, "Would you believe it?" and "Have you ever seen anything like that?" and "The frogs of today — what will they think of next?"

"Well," says the swimming teacher after a while, "you know what I think?"

"What?" ask all the grown-up frogs.

"I think, " says the swimming teacher, "that we finally taught Sam to swim."

ready, steady, read!